Nothing Wee About Me!

To Mom and Dad, for teaching me that it's what's on the inside that counts.
And to Julia, for sparking Liesel to life.
—K. C.

For my mom, who taught me how to be brave in the face of any scalawag
pirate, fire-breathing dragon, or rumbling volcano I might encounter.
It was the greatest lesson a wee girl could ask for.
—L. B.

Text copyright © 2019 Kim Chaffee
Illustrations copyright © 2019 Laura Bobbiesi

First published in 2019 by Page Street Kids,
an imprint of
Page Street Publishing Co.
27 Congress Street, Suite 105
Salem, MA 01970
www.pagestreetpublishing.com

Distributed by Macmillan, sales in Canada by The Canadian Manda Group

19 20 21 22 23 CCO 5 4 3 2 1

ISBN-13: 978-1-62414-692-3
ISBN-10: 1-62414-692-9

CIP data for this book is available from the Library of Congress.

This book was typeset in Bitter.
The illustrations were done in watercolor and ink.

Printed and bound in Shenzhen, Guangdong, China.

Page Street Publishing uses only materials from suppliers who are committed to
responsible and sustainable forest management.

Page Street Publishing protects our planet by donating to nonprofits like The Trustees,
which focuses on local land conservation.

Nothing Wee About Me!

A Magical Adventure by Kim Chaffee

illustrated by Laura Bobbiesi

PAGE STREET KIDS

It was finally Sunday again, and
Liesel had one thing on her mind:

ADVENTURE!

Liesel rushed through Grandma Rose's front door and into the kitchen. She shoved aside the spoons and spatulas and hurled the wire whisk.

"Looking for this?" asked Grandma Rose.

"Yes!" cheered Liesel.

"Dear Liesel, you're just like me when I was a *wee* girl."

"YOU KNOW THERE'S NOTHING WEE ABOUT ME, right, Grandma?"

"Of course not, dear Liesel. Of course not."

"Now, just a word of warning.
This old ladle doesn't work as well as it used to."

"Don't worry, Grandma.
It's always worked perfectly for me."

"Glad to hear it, dear. How about a hug
before you rush off on your next adventure?
And be back in time for Sunday soup."

Liesel wrapped Grandma Rose in the
biggest squeeze. "I promise."

Pointing the ladle toward the sky,
she took a deep breath and made her wish.

When Liesel opened her eyes, she was deep in
the ocean. She aimed her ladle-scope at an island
ahead and spotted a giant volcano.

It shuddered and sputtered.
It rumbled and boomed. It was going to blow!
But no one on the island seemed to notice.

"I must warn the villagers!" She steered her submarine toward land and sped ahead.

Liesel scurried across the sand toward town.
"Not so fast, wee girl," a pirate sneered.
"This here island belongs to me."

"But Captain," insisted Liesel, "that volcano is gonna blow
and destroy the whole island and . . .

THERE'S NOTHING WEE ABOUT ME!"

She jabbed her ladle-hook at the pirate.
"Let me pass, you scalawag, or prepare for a swashbuckling battle!"

"Yar! A brave buccaneer!" cried the pirate, shocked by Liesel's courage.
He turned on his heels and retreated across the beach.

Liesel ran through the village,
knocking on every door.

BANG! BANG! BANG!

"The lava is coming! The lava is coming!"

BANG! BANG! BANG!

"Get to the rescue boat!"

BANG! BANG! BANG!
"Open up! Open up!"
The door creaked, and
Liesel looked up.

Way . . .

way . . .

way up.

"Go away, *wee* girl," the dragon roared.
"Or join the prince as a prisoner in my castle."

"Not a chance, Dragon," snapped Liesel.
"There won't *be* a castle once that volcano goes *kablooey*!
AND THERE'S NOTHING **WEE** ABOUT ME!"

Liesel sliced her ladle-sword at the dragon.
"Let the prince go, you fire-breathing bully,
or it'll be you who gets roasted!"

"Ahhh! A mighty knight!" cried the dragon,
startled by Liesel's boldness.
He released his prisoner and shrank back into the castle.

Lava oozed from the volcano.
Coconuts tumbled from the trees.
Time was running out!
They'd never make it to the rescue boat now.
Liesel needed a new plan.

Pointing the ladle toward the sky,
she took a deep breath and made her wish.

"That is *not* a campfire!" Liesel shouted at the ladle. "And this is no time for s'mores!"

"Actually, I *could* use a snack," said the prince.

BOOM! RUMBLE! CRACK!

The prince winced. "Never mind! I can wait!"

Liesel tried again. . . .

"A plunger?!" Liesel grumbled. "How's this supposed to stop the volcano from exploding?"

The prince blushed.
"Umm, I have to go to the bathroom."

"You should have gone before we left the castle!" Liesel scolded.

BOOM! RUMBLE! CRACK!

She shook the ladle and tried again.
"Oh no, Grandma Rose was right!
This thing is busted!"

Liesel tried one last time. . . .

"Fishing?" the prince peeped. "Now?"

"Yes!" Liesel cheered.

BOOM! RUMBLE! CRACK!

She hooked the largest coconut she could find
and cast her line higher and farther than ever before.

The prince was not convinced. "I can't watch!"

YIPEE! WAHOO! HOORAY!
Everyone danced and cheered.
Liesel wished she could stay but
Grandma Rose was waiting.

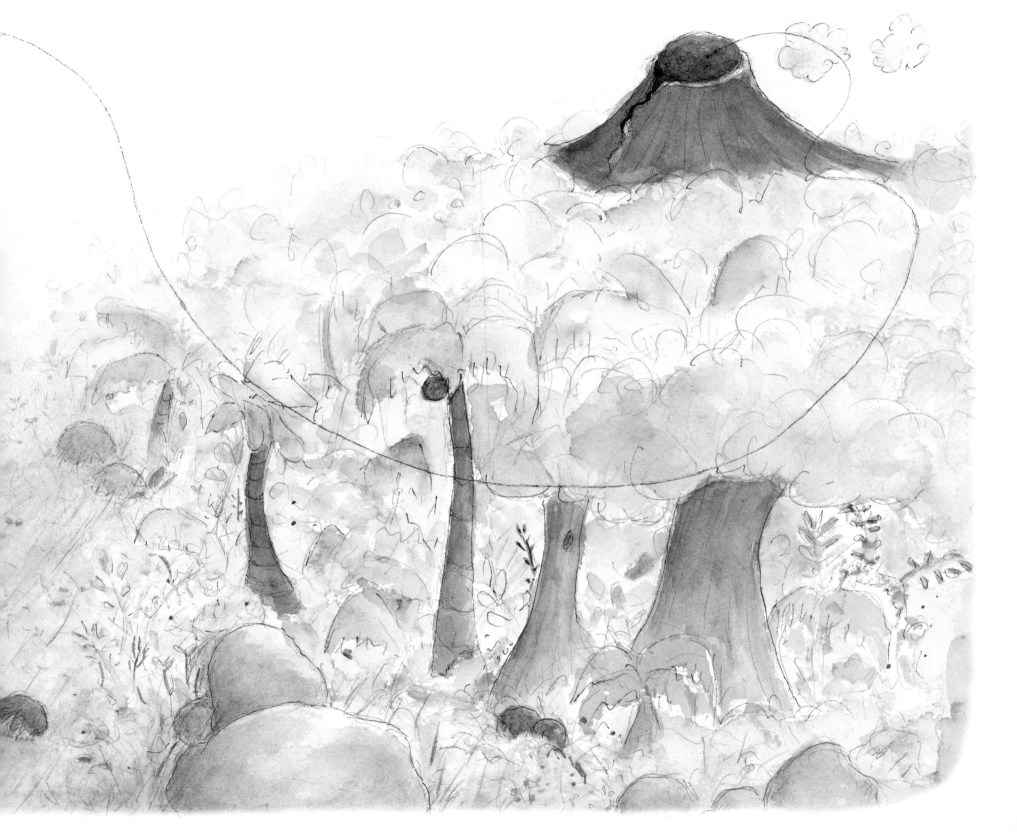

Tilting her bowl, Liesel slurped every last sip.

Grandma Rose served up another helping.
"I've never seen you eat so much Sunday soup, dear.
That must have been some adventure today!"

"The best one yet," Liesel said between spoonfuls.

"I hope it wasn't too dangerous," Grandma Rose said, worried.

Liesel stopped eating and stood up.

"NOTHING THIS **WEE** GIRL COULDN'T HANDLE."